1. Three Nights Later — 3
2. The Soukouyan on the Roof — 9
3. The Mama Glo at Deep Blue — 14
4. The Jumbie in Elvira's House — 21
5. The Soukouyan from Marie Galante — 27
6. The House that Baptiste Built — 32
7. Tax and the Cemetery Spirit — 36
8. Rufus and the La Diabless — 43
9. Mabel and the de Laurence Ring — 47
10. How Heskit and Petite Killed a Soukouyan — 53
11. Glossary of Terms — 61

Three Nights Later

The night was quiet as if the whole world was holding its breath, waiting for something to happen. The moon looked so big and hung so low, it appeared as if you could reach out and touch it. Somewhere in the distance, a dog howled mournfully and even further away an owl hooted eerily.

Those were not good signs for Mama. She made a sign of the cross before huddling me into the living room. On her face, she wore the look which told me she was worried. I knew what it was all about.

It has been three nights since Mr. James died and Mama had always told me that a person never knows death had come until three nights later. "You will die today eh but you will not know until three nights after," she always said. Then the spirit would make one last move around the place it used to live as a human being before heading in the direction of the cemetery to meet the physical body buried there.

And tonight was the night Mr. James was going to know that he had died.

Whenever someone died in our area, Mama was the first person who was called, "to take care of things." Then she would grab her rosary, a small bottle of holy water that never seemed to run dry, her book of novenas and hurry as fast as her legs could carry her to the death house. There she would chant some psalms, sprinkle holy water in the four corners of the house, place coins over the dead person's eyes to keep them closed, say her rosary, repeat prayers from the novena book and wait for the funeral home to come and pick up the body.

Mama said her job was to keep evil spirits from contaminating the body of the dead person because if they did, the person would not truly die but return to work with obeah men and do all sorts of evil things. She saw herself as the last stance between the evil world and the living world.

But despite her familiarity with death, Mama was afraid of spirits, jumbies, lougawous, soukouyans and the like. Her fear was evident all over our house: brooms were left upside down to prevent soukouyans from stealing them to fly around at night. Crucifixes adorned every window and door; a horseshoe hung upside down on the main door to prevent soukouyans from entering; the walls were covered with images of St. Michael the Archangel and St. George slaying the dragon. Then there were things that Mama had in the house which I was not allowed to see. I heard her talk about them, however. They included cemetery dirt, a maho piman whip and the teeth of a male pig.

So naturally when Mr. James died Mama went to perform her duties and I followed. This was the first time I had actually gone with Mama to a death house. Upon arrival, the air and place were punctuated by cries of anguish. A solemn look covered everyone's face.

We entered the house and into the bedroom. The smell of death filled my nostrils; a heavy, pungent and suffocating smell. Mr. James lay on his bed as if sleeping. In his hands, he grasped a crucifix undoubtedly place there by a relative. His eyes were still open, staring at nothing and he appeared as white as a sheet. For even a six-year-old like me, what I saw was clear evidence that he was dead.

Mama placed coins over Mr. James' eyes and began her rituals but I could not take my eyes off the corpse on the bed and, suddenly a terrifying fear filled me. I could feel my head growing bigger and bigger and my tongue getting heavier and heavier. I was struggling for breath.

Mama's chanting, the cries of sorrow, the wind in the breadfruit tree outside all blended into one and seemed to grow louder and louder. Then everything around me started growing dark and Mama's chanting, the cries of sorrow, the wind all seemed to grow fainter and fainter. Dark shadows danced in front of my eyes and breathing became laborious. Then to my utter horror, Mr. James turned his head, the coins dropped off and he winked at me. The last thing I remembered was a weak scream coming from my mouth and then everything turned pitch black.

When I came to my senses I was at home in bed with Mama peering down at me. I tried to get up and felt weak. Mama gently pushed me back and said, "You got sick and passed out. I had to carry you home."

"I was not sick, Mama," I objected. "Mr. James winked at me. I saw it, he winked at me."

A look of deep concern suddenly appeared on Mama's face. "You sure you know what you talking about?" she whispered, half comfortingly, half puzzled.

I nodded gravely.

Then Mama immediately sprang into action. First, I was anointed with olive oil. That night, I was awakened at midnight and given a bath which consisted of Glory Cedar, Ponm Koulie, Zèb Kouwès, and Tabak Zombie leaves. Added to this was Red Lavender and Alcalado.

Then Mama told me what had transpired. She said Mr. James' body was about to be taken over by an evil spirit but she had arrived in time, however, she was not sure how powerful the spirit was and if it had completely taken over his body. When I saw Mr. James open his eyes and wink at me, it was the work of the evil spirit, she said and she was sure it would come after me knowing that I was a weak and vulnerable child. "But doh worry your head," she concluded. "I know how to take care of things."

In the distance, the dog kept howling and Mama walked around straightening things in the house unnecessarily. The story she told me about what happened at Mr. James' house had evoked a combination of fear and curiosity in me and somehow I wished Papa was home.

Papa had gone to say the rosary at the death house which was normally done for nine days after a person died. Papa was a brave man who feared no man or spirit and the talks of Mr. James' spirit did not put a dent in his fearless demeanor. Papa loved rosary recitals and Nine Nights because it was a time to meet old friends, drink some rum and have a good time.

"That damn dog there doesn't shut its mouth then," Mama said as the dog kept howling in the distance. "I wish I could give it a kick in it bottom eh."

Mama went to the kitchen and suddenly I got the sensation that someone was outside the window. A moment later, the strange but familiar smell of death filled my nostrils.

The smell brought back a flood of memories from Mr. James' house; Mama's chanting, the wails of sorrow, the wind in the breadfruit tree. I felt my head getting bigger and bigger and my chest closed around my lungs. Then I felt as if someone or something was pulling me towards the window. I tried to struggle but it was an attempt at futility as I felt myself being dragged closer and closer to it. By now the smell of death was overpowering and it seemed to envelop me in a cocoon of which there was no return.

Before I knew it I was standing at the window, looking out. Outside was like daylight and the howling of the dog had stopped. Thick silence covered everything. The smell of death was so powerful that I wanted to vomit.

And then I saw it, standing below the window. I only saw the top part of the body, from the chest up. It appeared as if it had no legs but was just floating in mid-air. The hair was matted as if by water and the eyes stared out at nothing. It was Mr. James!

For what seemed like an eternity I stared at the specter. On my part, I could not think or move or say anything. It appeared as if I was held, bound by some invisible force over which I had no control. I tried to scream but my tongue had turned to lead and nothing emanated from my mouth. I tried to move back but it seemed as if my legs had stopped working.

I struggled desperately and in a strong surge of energy, I heard myself screaming, "Mama, Mama."

From somewhere far, far away I heard hurried footsteps and then felt Mama's strong and comforting embrace enveloping me. She told me the next day that my eyes were turning white and I was foaming at the mouth when she found me at the window. But that night I didn't know all this and Mama took me to the bed while she repeated over and over again her favorite Latin Prayer, "Veni Creator Spiritus." I was given a glass of water and Mama asked me what happened.

I told her and her face became chiseled with determination.

She left me on the bed and went to the window. "I rebuke you, you evil spirit," Mama said. "I rebuke you in the name of the Infant Jesus of Prague."

She returned to the bedroom and told me she was going to do what had to be done because she said an evil spirit had somehow entered Mr. James's dead body and was now trying to take control of it. The evil spirit has somehow locked itself onto me and was trying to possess me, a living body, instead of Mr. James' dead body.

The revelation filled me with horror. I sat trembling on the bed as Mama made preparations to battle the spirit which she said was still outside.

First, she made sure her clothes were inside out, she then wrapped her left sleeve three times, spun around three times and poured a handful of the cemetery dirt over her head. Then she opened an old suitcase from the corner and pulled out the Maho Piman whip. I had never seen it before and the sight of it filled me with a mixture of awe and curiosity. "Stay there," Mama whispered hoarsely to me and went outside.

That night I didn't know what really happened outside. I stayed on the bed filled with fear and shaking like a leaf in a hurricane. All I heard was Mama screaming strange incantations and the crackling of the Maho Piman whip. This went on for about ten minutes but it seemed like an eternity. Suddenly there was a loud blood curling scream and then silence.

The silence was so heavy; I could hear my heart beating and the sound of my strenuous breathing.

Finally, Mama came in exhausted. She carefully wrapped the Maho Piman whip and placed it back in the suitcase.

She came and laid down beside me and whispered that everything was going to be fine. We laid silently on the bed for a long time unable to move, trying to comprehend what transpired that night.

And then somewhere outside a cricket started chirping merrily.

"That is a good sign eh," Mama whispered. "A very good sign."

The Soukouyan on the Roof

It all began one moonless country night long before the advent of electricity in our part of Dominica.

It was one of those nights in which everything appeared to be abnormal: the wind blew mournfully through the big mango tree behind our house, the usual joyful crescendo of the crickets and other night creatures was muffled and unenthusiastic. In the distance, the restless Atlantic Ocean crashed unusually loud on the shoreline. Even the lone kerosene lamp in our living room appeared tired -- I got the impression it would die at any moment.

My older brother and I were in our room about to fall asleep when we first heard it. At the beginning, it was rather faint but it grew slightly louder with each moment.

"You hear that?" my brother whispered softly. I nodded in the dark and whispered, "What you think it is?" He didn't respond. It continued for about three minutes, maybe less. Then abruptly as it began, it stopped.

The sound we heard was hard to describe. My brother would later say it sounded as if a crab was crawling across the galvanized roof. I thought it sounded as if someone was using fingernails and scraping the roof or a branch rubbing against it.

Whatever the cause of the scratching, crawling sound, it was drastic enough for Mammy and Daddy to hold a whispering conference in the kitchen the next morning while we stayed outside straining our ears to hear what they were talking about. When my brother tried to enter the kitchen to give his opinion Mammy snapped, "chil' doh push yourself in big people business."

Then in a grave voice, and gesticulating extravagantly, Mammy related the night's episode over the hibiscus hedge to our neighbor Misilda. After that, the news spread through the area quickly. Everyone began arriving at our house offering counsel.

"Somebody playing something on all u eh," our uncle said.

Another uncle concluded that people were getting jealous over Daddy's banana field and were working some obeah on him. One of Mammy's favorite gossip partners pointed out that Mammy's friendly disposition was causing jealousy among other women and she was being targeted by something evil.

But it was the opinion of a fellah who went by the name of Kong that sent shockwaves through everyone. "I tell all you is a soukouyan eh," he stated. A heavy silence fell over everyone which was only broken when Kong cleared his throat and said, "All you doh have a rum there then? I so thirsty I could drink a whole bottle I telling all you."

Since we were not allowed in 'big people's business,' we consulted Zabef, a distant cousin, for advice. Although she was barely twelve and just two years older than I was, Zabef knew everything. It was she who told us that the Catholic church near our school was always full of jumbies at nights and Father Gary would have conversations with them. Because of that, we avoided the church as much as we could, even in broad daylight. When Father Gary came to our school for devotions, we avoided him and pray that he didn't come to shake our hands.

It was Zabef who told us that a Mama Glo (mermaid) lived in the big pool near the mouth of the river which was our favorite swimming spot. But she told us we need not fear as long as we didn't repeat 'mama glo' three times aloud or in our minds, or didn't sit with our backs facing the river.

She told us many stories of jumbies, and la diabless and lougawous, which instilled great fear in us.

But Zabef's favorite foray into the depth of our fears was her details of 'la feh di moun' (the end of the world). It was going to be a time of great famine, and wars and suffering. Then all the dead would rise, even Mattaius who drowned in the sea and whose body was never found. And Jesus would appear on a cloud in the heavens among great lightning and thunder to take away all good people while bad people were taken by the devil. The story evoked great dread in us and Zabef demanded ice pops or Shirley Biscuit or coconut tablets in exchange for not telling us.

So it was from Zabef we got our first real lesson on soukouyans. She said they were women who turned into blood sucking, evil creatures and who flew around at night, sometimes in the form of a huge fireball or a big firefly that was common in the area, which we used to call 'lalo.'

"So when all you see a lalo, all you have to careful eh," she cautioned. "Not all lalo is real lalo." Because of that, we feared lalos greatly and whenever they were seen, they were caught by older children and killed.

In order to become a soukouyan, the woman had to peel off her skin and place it in a mortar or 'pilon.' Then she would mount a broomstick and fly away, sometimes as far as England but their most favorite destination was Haiti. "That is where they go and kiss the devil bottom," Zabef pointed out. But they liked sticking around the area, sucking people's blood, listening to people's conversations at night and creating a general evil atmosphere.

"It easy to know who is a soukouyan eh," Zabef stated. "If you see a woman always talking to herself, always walking on the left side of the road and she fraid to pass by the church, she is a soukouyan."

That night with a mixture of fear and excitement my brother and I waited for our uninvited visitor. But we were ready as instructed by Zabef: a crucifix and a string of garlic adorned our window, our clothes were on inside out and back to front and each of us wore a rosary around our necks. To top it off before going to bed we both sucked on green limes. "That will turn all your blood sour and if the soukouyan suck all you, it must vomit the blood," Zabef enlightened us.

We waited and we waited but the night was only accentuated by the familiar sound of the wind in the mango tree, the crickets outside and the crashing of the Atlantic Ocean against the shore.

Eventually, we drifted into sleep. That happened the following night and then the next, followed by the next and we did not hear the sound. Slowly the crucifix and the garlic went down. We forgot to put on our clothes back to front and inside out and the lime tasted sourer every night and we gave that up also. The sound on the roof became like some distant dream, far back in memory.

Then one night, as abruptly as the first time, we heard it again. This time, it was over our parent's bedroom. Our blood froze and I held on to my brother in pure horror. To our utter amazement, Mammy got out of her bed and spoke and there was anger in her voice.

"What I do all you?" she demanded. "Eh? What I do all you? I doh take all you man, I doh jealous all you thing. What all you want on my house? But Mother Mary, what I do those people there nuh? What they want with me? Leave my house alone eh. Just leave it."

She fell silent briefly before starting up again, swearing that she was going to say a Novena in honor of Our Lady of Fatima and was going as far as Portsmouth to find a priest to say a mass for her. "And I know people that know how to do things eh," she stated. "I know people".

The next day our parents wore a grave look on their faces and the plot was hatched to get rid of the soukouyan. We got all the details from Zabef. Daddy had gone to Londel for advice since he was versed in the ways of the soukouyan. Daddy was instructed to get a horse shoe and nail it upside down over the main entrance to our house. Then he was to build a fish gun of Mahaut wood. The spear of the fish gun was to be rubbed with garlic and alkali. When Daddy heard the soukouyan on the roof he was to get up quietly, undress and exit the house backward, as naked as he was born. Then he was to fire the fish gun in the direction of the sound.

"That will be the end of it," Londel promised.

That night our parents gathered us together and told us what was to transpire. "And I doh want to hear a word from all you," Mammy warned fiercely. "Not a word."

That night we waited. And so the following night. Nothing happened.

About two weeks later our hearts leaped into our throat as we heard the scraping sound again. The soukouyan was back!!

We held our breath and we strained our ears to hear what was happening. Daddy got quietly off his bed and with light footsteps headed to the door. We heard the door open silently. And there was a loud "twang" as the rubber that sent the fish gun's spear to its target was released. Daddy quickly and quietly entered the house, closed the door and we heard something that sounded like the shuffling of busy feet behind our house. And silence, unbearable silence.

The spear from the fish gun was never found despite extensive searches by Daddy the next day. Neither did we see any blood trail as promised by Zabef. But one thing was sure, we never heard the sound on our roof again.

The Mama Glo at Deep Blue

The allure of Deep Blue was overwhelming and powerful.

Deep Blue was a huge basin of water carved out by the swift-flowing Mapo River, creating a perfect natural pool for anyone who had a passion for a cold river swim.

The river cascaded into a frothy white substance in the pool, quieten down by the time it reached the middle and became mirror-like by the time it reached the other end. The water itself was crystal clear and cold to the touch. In the middle section of the pool, where it was deepest, the water looked bluish, hence its name. Trees hung over the pool and their branches made perfect spots for the adventurous who wanted to dive into the delicious water.

Speculations varied on the exact depth of Deep Blue and although competitions were held to reach its bottom, no one had actually accomplished such a feat.

Deep Blue was popular among the grownups but mostly on weekends. People did their laundry there, sometimes spent their entire day there cooking, roasting breadfruit or cooking pots; people caught crabs, crayfish and a tiny fish called 'lush' there.

But most of all, Deep Blue was very, very popular among school children because it was located in a remote valley, away from everything, making it the perfect spot for those wanting to skip school and spend an afternoon of freedom away from the rigors of Mathematics, Social Studies, and Penmanship. Many of these students left home in their uniforms but sneaked extra clothes in their bags for their Deep Blue escapade and returned home in the afternoons innocent enough, again in their uniforms.

But despite the popularity of Deep Blue, there were whispers that it was the home of a Mama Glo. People said that somehow, it was connected to the sea, although the sea was miles away. There was a tunnel, they said, and that tunnel was used by the Mama Glo to travel between Deep Blue and the open ocean. As if to support this theory, whenever the sea was rough, Deep Blue would heave restlessly as if some strange creature lay in its depth struggling to free itself.

However, these things about Deep Blue were not spoken of openly. They were just whispered among people as if the mentioning of them aloud would disrupt the delicate balance existing between humans and the Mama Glo that lived in or used Deep Blue.

This did not deter the throngs of students who rushed to Deep Blue after school, neither did it prevent those who skipped school altogether from splashing in it all afternoon long.

The reason for this fearlessness was that they had their defense against the Mama Glo. First of all, you never, ever sit with your back facing Deep Blue. Such a position made it easier for the Mama Glo to sneak up on you and snatch you and take you to the depth with it. But most importantly you never think of the words 'Mama Glo' once in your head. If by accident you did so, you simply had to repeat the words three times in quick succession and you would be safe.

And so Deep Blue remained popular with school children until Cha Bruney became head teacher.

Cha Bruney was a firm adherent of discipline and a staunch believer in the virtues of the whip and in a gross manipulation of the age old proverb, he once proclaimed that "the whip is mightier than the sword." His favorite whips were made from guava branches and he used them liberally.

One of Cha Bruney's first edicts as head teacher was a total ban on Deep Blue. During assembly one morning, he said anyone who was caught going to Deep Blue, was caught at Deep Blue or even harbored the thought of going to Deep Blue, would be punished. Not even the little ones in Grade One were exempt, Cha Bruney said, because the rule applied to everyone, "from captain down to cook."

The restriction lasted probably for a week and the trickle of students who sneaked away for a swim slowly turned into a torrent. Cha Bruney's guava whips were kept busy but a brilliant kid came up with the idea of stuffing cardboard in his pants' behind as a guard against the sting of the whip and soon the technique was widely duplicated.

Realizing that his whip was having no impact, Cha Bruney called a PTA meeting and preached on the evils of a non-educated society and according to him, Deep Blue was standing in the way of the students under his watch from obtaining a proper education. Then he told the gathered parents that he had some ideas about making Deep Blue unattractive and non-inviting. The most outrageous idea was diverting the river through a small nearby channel bypassing Deep Blue altogether. This did not go down well with many parents. Soon the meeting degenerated into a Babel of opposing ideas but Cha Bruney's strong will won everyone over and his proposal was given serious consideration.

That was when strange things began happening.

First of all, that night the sea became violently rough. All night long people listened as huge waves crashed against the seashore in loud thunderous claps and the next day fishermen rushed to the beach in order to save their boats from the angry ocean. They sat and watched in amazement as monstrous swells pummeled the beach relentlessly, sending huge plumes of white spray into the air. Even seasoned fishermen shook their heads in disbelief at this occurrence and wondered what was going on. They said the last time the sea was that rough was during the passage of Hurricane David and they could blame the hurricane, but what they were witnessing had no apparent cause.

Deep Blue itself became unapproachable as it frothed and heaved like a cauldron of angry boiling water and for the first time in a long time, the valley in which it was located was devoid of happy laughter and the delightful squeals of children enjoying its delectable waters.

The sea remained rough for three days and concerns began growing among the fishermen about the source of their livelihood. On the third day a fisherman who went by the name 'Duck' decided he could not take it any longer and was going out to sea no matter what. People said the sea flowed through Duck's veins and he was more comfortable on it or in it rather than on dry land. His swimming capabilities were legendary, hence his nickname, and he had survived many bruising encounters with the sea.

Duck ignored the wise counsel of the other fishermen who took his decision so seriously that they refused to help him push his boat to the frothing sea. He painstakingly and singlehandedly pushed the boat to the sea's edge and waited for a slight break in the huge waves to push it and go waterborne. When he thought he saw a break, Duck pushed the boat with all his might into the raging waters.

Duck was a good boatsman. He skillfully maneuvered the boat through the waves steering the boat parallel to them and at the last moment he made the boat face the waves headlong and he sliced through them like a knife through butter. Despite this, the boat was tossed around violently like a toy and sometimes it seemed as if it would be swamped completely.

Those on shore looked on with amazement and fear as Duck's boat battled the furious waters and it appeared he would eventually make it through to deeper waters where the sea was less angry. But then as if out of nowhere, a huge wave arose. Those who looked on said it was probably the biggest they had ever seen. The wave towered over the others with white spray streaming from its crest.

The hearts of the people on shore sank and they began shouting frantically over the roar of the sea to alert Duck. The wave grew bigger and bigger and as if in slow motion, crashed unto itself, emitting a loud thunderous clap. The entire sea was left in a white, frothy mess and this completely engulfed Duck and his boat.

It was then people saw the Mama Glo or got a glimpse of it. All they really saw was a flash of its golden hair and seconds later, its bluish green fish tail appeared right over Duck's boat. Then both the boat and the Mama Glo disappeared, while the people on shore stood horrified at what was unfolding before them.

Then the sea grew rougher and everyone had to retreat to higher grounds. Night fell quickly and everyone went to their homes. That night, no one could sleep because the sea howled and raged nonstop like a captured monster. Everyone felt helpless in the face of Duck's demise and they wished he had listened to them and not face the raging sea alone.

The following day, abruptly as it started, the raging of the sea subsided and a search party was immediately organized for Duck but despite an extensive search of the shoreline for more than a week, the sea refused to give up his body.

The incident traumatized everyone and talks of the Mama Glo were on everybody's lips for many weeks after that.

A couple of weeks later, Edward was in the valley on a crab and crayfish catching expedition. It was not a good afternoon as the crabs and crayfish were scarce and he was getting frustrated. By late afternoon he was approaching Deep Blue and suddenly he heard the sound of soft singing. Edward was baffled by this because sometimes the sound seemed to be coming from all directions but most of the times from up the river, in the direction of Deep Blue. The sound itself was soft, enticing, inviting and seemed to dominate the gentle sound of the flowing river.

Filled with curiosity Edward crept toward the sound, getting closer and closer to Deep Blue. As he drew closer it seemed nothing else mattered but that sweet singing sound. It dominated his thoughts, his being, and his very action.

Almost mechanically, he felt himself being pulled to the source of the singing. Eventually, he peered over the last rock and sitting on a huge stone on the edge of Deep Blue, was the Mama Glo.

It seems as if it didn't sense Edward's presence because it just sat there combing its long golden hair with a comb that appeared to be made out of solid gold. Its bluish-green fishtail glistened in the faint sunlight and the color of the skin, on the upper part of the body, was pale white. Then suddenly it stopped singing and only the gentle sound of the river punctuated the silence.

Edward did not know how long he stood there staring at the unusual spectacle but then all of a sudden his feet slid on the stone he was standing on and landed in the water with a loud splash.

The splash shattered the silence and the Mama Glo spun around bewildered and locked eyes with Edward. The eyes were fiery emerald green and displayed no emotions. The face looked human enough although Edward somehow knew that it was incapable of smiling or laughing. The lips were thin and pale as if no blood flowed through them and the nose was equally thin.

Edward turned and ran like he had never run before. The only sound he heard behind him was a loud splash as the Mama Glo dove back into the depths of Deep Blue.

Soon everyone was talking about Edward's sighting of the Mama Glo at Deep Blue and the whole matter was gaining legendary status. Everyone believed the story, everyone but Cha Bruney.

Cha Bruney thought the whole thing was a conspiracy to prevent his re-routing of the river around Deep Blue and so he was determined to continue as planned.

Cha Bruney did not believe in stories of Mama Glo, soukouyan, la diabless, lougawous and the like. He thought they were stories made up by ignorant, uneducated people who did not want to enjoy the beauty of knowledge and wisdom. He would shrug them off as "legends" and "creole folk tales."

So one day he went down to Deep Blue to draw the plan for the re-routing of the river. When he arrived, Deep Blue lay quiet and was smooth as a mirror. He pulled out his tape to start measuring the new river route.

Then, he felt as if someone was watching him and when he looked up, the Mama Glo was sitting on the same huge stone that Edward had seen it sitting on. For a couple of seconds, Cha Bruney's brain refused to process what his eyes were seeing and he thought someone was playing a stupid trick on him.

But the apparition before him would not go away and slowly it began penetrating the fog of his disbelief. And then he felt his body growing limp and in defiance of the rules of gravity, he felt himself being lifted from the ground by a strange invisible force. Cha Bruney floated over the ground in the grip of the force and was taken right over Deep Blue. Then the force released him and he felt himself tumbling towards the water.

All the time, the Mama Glo sat on the stone, unmoving, its emerald green eyes emotionless like that of a snake.

Cha Bruney's measuring tape was found near Deep Blue where he had dropped it but his body was never found.

After that, Deep Blue never returned to its glorious self because it became filled with stones and dirt. Some people blamed this on deforestation upstream but for a couple of days during the hurricane season when the sea was rough, the stones and dirt would mysteriously disappear and Deep Blue would heave restlessly. But this lasted only for a couple of days and soon the stones and dirt would return.

And on a full moon night, if one is within hearing range of Deep Blue, the singing of the Mama Glo can be heard to this day.

The jumbie in Elvira's house

When Elvira hit her big toe in her yard one Friday afternoon, she knew it was not a good sign.

Fridays were not good days because on those days soukouyans could 'hear' what you were thinking, malfétès plotted their evil plans, lougawous planned their weekend sojourns and la diabless targeted their next victims. Additionally, jumbies normally left the refuge of the woods to haunt people and their homes.

Knowing this, Elvira made a sign of the cross, spat to the four corners of the earth and gathered three handfuls of dirt which she threw behind her before entering her house.

When Elvira examined her toe, she realized the skin had completely fallen off and the red flesh was clearly visible. Cursing under her breath she washed the toe completely, threw MB Powder over it and tied it securely with a white piece of cloth. The toe continued to throb and Elvira resorted to drinking two Phensic tablets before heading to bed.

That night she had the first of a series of strange dreams. In it, she was walking through a forest of bwa dyab and the branches were all trying to get her. She ran and ran. Then she noticed a little old man running after her. She could see it was a man but somehow she could not see his features. It was as if some parts of him were invisible or hidden behind a thick fog.

The more she ran, the more the old man kept gaining on her and finally he caught up with her, grabbed her foot and slammed her toe against a rock. The pain was excruciating and Elvira woke up clutching at her toe and to her surprise, the white cloth was gone, so was the MB Powder. Only the bright red flesh showed.

She stumbled out of bed, searching for the piece of cloth but it was nowhere to be found. Greatly puzzled, she added more MB Powder to the toe, got a fresh piece of cloth, bound it firmly and returned to bed.

She was just about to fall asleep when she heard the whisper, "Elvira, Elvira." Twice. No more.

The whisper came from the window above her head and she was about to respond but held back because she knew that when you hear your name called out only twice in the night, it has to be a jumbie.

Elvira suddenly felt cold. Goosebumps appeared all over her body. She shivered and drew the sheet closer. Then she felt as if she was bound by some invisible force. She tried to move but she could not. She remained motionless on her bed in that state for a couple minutes until the odd feeling slowly drifted away. She jumped from her bed uttering some choice words in the process. She grabbed her rosary and repeated it until she fell asleep.

The next day Elvira related the previous night's proceedings to her friend Valda and Valda muttered, "Something not right eh, something not right."

That afternoon while Elvira was cleaning underneath the house, to her great surprise, she found the white piece of cloth that bound her toe the previous night.

"But how that get there nuh?" she asked herself. She tormented her brains trying to figure out how the cloth got underneath the house and finally she came to the conclusion that maybe it was taken by a rat that was attracted to the scent of her blood.

That night Elvira took out her bible, dusted it and was about to start reading it when she heard a loud fluttering outside. Thinking a chicken must have lost its way in the dark she opened the window and said, "shoo shoo. Come out of the yard." The fluttering stopped and she was about to close the window when she saw a dark shadow under the breadfruit tree in the yard. She peered through the darkness, straining to see who the shadow belonged to.

"Hendrie, you that there?" she asked. Hendrie was a guy around the area who had 'lost his head' and was known to exhibit strange behavior. But the shadow remained unmoving.

"Hendrie, you that there?" she repeated and when the shadow remained unmoving she said, "If you doh come out from there, I will throw pee pee on you eh."

But the shadow remained unmoving and suddenly Elvira realized it resembled the old man from her dream and she felt cold. She quickly closed the window and once again she got the strange feeling that she was being held down by some invisible force. She fought and she struggled against the strange force but it was no use. When it finally released her, she found herself on the floor and then her toe began throbbing.

She never slept that night because the pain in her toe was excruciating.

The next day Valda helped Elvira untie the toe, cleaned it properly and this time, they splashed mercurochrome over the wound before adding the MB Powder. The pain continued and they decided to leave the toe untied.

Then Elvira told Valda what had transpired the night before and Valda listened with great interest, scratching her head occasionally. "Something not right eh, something not right," she kept repeating.

Suddenly Elvira felt a sharp pain in her wounded toe and she cried out in agony. Her sudden cry startled Valda who rushed to her side. "My toe, my toe," Elvira cried as a sharp pain stabbed through it. She pointed to the toe and as the two looked on, the MB Powder started moving as if something was under it.

And to their utter horror, the head of a sour fly emerged from under the MB Powder and slowly the entire fly wiggled out and dropped to the floor.

"Where it come from, where it come from," Elvira shouted.

"I doh know, I doh know," Valda shouted back. The two sat transfixed as the sour fly, covered with MB Powder, crawled aimlessly around and suddenly Valda stamped her foot over it, killing it instantly.

The two sat quietly for a long time unable to comprehend what they had just witnessed.

Valda was the first to speak. "That toe there is not a good toe eh," she said gravely. "You notice since you get that toe there plenty things happening."

And so the decision was made to visit a gardé to get his opinion on what was going on.

A small bald man, the gardé listened intently while he scribbled in a small white book. When he heard about the sour fly coming out of the toe, he dropped his book and appeared suddenly concerned. "Somebody put something in your house," he stated. "Is a jumbie somebody put there and we have to run it away."

The next day Valda and Elvira took a bus to Roseau to buy what was prescribed by the gardé. The list consists of a black candle, a red candle, Oil of Protection, Stay Away Powder, Oil of Never Return, All Purpose Incense, Banishing Powder, among others.

They had to wait when the moon was in its first quarter before they could start the ritual that would drive the jumbie away from Elvira's house and when the time came the gardé arrived at around 11:00 p.m. The whole thing was to begin at midnight.

First, he anointed the black and red candles with the Oil of Protection and Oil of Never Return. Then he sprinkled the Banishing Powder and Stay Away Powder in a circle around the house. And he and Valda and Elvira waited for midnight.

Suddenly there was a loud bang outside and the house began shaking. The gardé motioned for silence and said they should not be distracted by anything. He quickly sprinkled Stay Away Powder over everyone and lit the black candle. He placed it in the middle of the room and took the red candle. He spun around three times then lit it and placed it next to the black candle. He then lit the All Purpose incense and placed a stick at each corner of the house.

The banging outside continued and then the front door flew open as if pushed by a fierce and violent wind. Elvira and Valda held on to each other in pure terror. The windows followed suit and all flew open, swinging crazily as if pushed by some angry invisible force. This was followed by loud sounds on the galvanized roof. At exactly midnight, the gardé opened his bag and pulled out his book of obeah. For the next minute or so he uttered words from it while the windows and door banged unceasingly.

Then without warning the gardé fell backward as if pushed violently. The obeah book went flying and the gardé landed in an unceremonial heap in the corner with a loud groan. He quickly got up, grabbed the obeah book again and continued his incantations.

In the next five minutes, everything grew quiet and it was then Elvira and Valda saw the jumbie. It was the same old man that had haunted Elvira's dreams. It stood for a second in the doorway as if unsure of what to do next. Then it released a scream, a scream that rang in their ears. Next, it turned and fled.

The gardé found a chair and sunk into it, completely exhausted. Valda and Elvira stayed frozen to their spots, clutching each other, afraid to move. They remained so until the next morning.

Just before the sun rose the gardé sprinkled more of the oils and powders around the house. He then washed and cleansed Elvira's toe.

He then told them the jumbie was an evil one that wanted to possess Elvira but would now never return. Elvira was to sprinkle the oils and powders around the house for seven days more, just to make sure the jumbie never came back.

And the toe healed quickly after that. As for the sour fly, Elvira has it to this day, suspended and preserved in a bottle of Macousherie Rum.

It was a reminder of the jumbie that haunted her and wanted to possess her.

The Soukouyan from Marie Galante

It all started a couple of months before Hurricane David in 1979 and Avandale was the first to see it.

Avandale always went to bed late because he ate dinner late and he would sit under the mango tree in his yard so that his "food could go dong" while he weaved straw baskets to sell to passing tourists.

From the northeastern part of Dominica where Avandale lived, Marie Galante was clearly visible, lying like a huge blue whale right across the ocean. The French island was so close that on a clear day one could see white sand beaches and at nights, headlamps of motor vehicles.

But that night, what Avandale saw in Marie Galante was no motor vehicle. It looked like a boukan (bonfire) with flames leaping in all directions. He knew Marie Galante was close but not so close as to see a boukan and if it were one, it would have to be a really big one to be seen so clearly all the way in Dominica.

Puzzled, Avandale dropped his basket and kept observing the boukan, but suddenly it went out and was replaced by what looked like the blue light of a flashlight. Soon, the blue light was replaced by a dim yellow light. That too eventually went off and was again replaced by the boukan with leaping flames. The flames were so bright that they cast an eerie reflection in the water.

Having never witnessed such a thing before Avandale forgot his work and kept observing the strange occurrence. After maybe half an hour the boukan leaped into the air, "like a helicopter taking off" he would later say, and started heading towards Dominica.

Amazed Avandale stood transfixed as the mysterious object drew closer and closer from across the ocean, but after a while it turned south, heading down in the direction of Grand Bay and Petite Savanne.

Suddenly he felt extraordinarily tired and Avandale stumbled to his bed and fell into deep slumber.

When he woke up the next day he was even more tired. And it was then he noticed the odd bluish dark spot on his left thigh. The area was slightly painful to the touch and Avandale tried to remember if he had knocked himself in that spot but he could not recall ever doing so. He rubbed the area with Iodex and decided to keep the previous night's event and the strange spot on his thigh to himself.

The following night the same thing happened; the boukan appeared in Marie Galante, the blue light followed by the dim yellow light, then the boukan leaped into the air and flew towards Dominica and then the overwhelming exhaustion. The next morning Avandale discovered more strange spots on his body and more Iodex was rubbed.

A few nights later Gibbs was on the latrine paying the price of two days of heavy cask rum drinking. All of a sudden the dark night turned bright as day and he peered through the door of the outhouse to see what was going on. On the breadfruit tree, he saw something he had never seen before. He later said what he saw resembled an old woman on the tree and it seems as if she was covered or surrounded by fire.

Filled with tremendous fright, Gibbs did not wait to see more but made a mad dash to his house, leaving his pants and underwear in the outhouse. He huddled in a corner for the rest of the night, to frightened to move even when his bowel freely relieved itself.

Too embarrassed to tell anyone of his experience, Gibbs kept it a secret. But there were stranger things to occur following the night Avandale first saw the peculiar light in Marie Galante.

One night Ma Balcooleh could not sleep because her dog had just given birth under the house and the newborn puppies kept whimpering unceasingly. After a couple hours of torment, she decided to move the litter to the kitchen which was some distance from the house. She grabbed a candle and went out in the pitch darkness. As she stepped outside, she noticed that Ma Johnson's house up the road was alive with light as if a party was taking place. She had never seen so much light at that house before but she shrugged off what she saw and proceeded to complete the task she had set out to do.

After the last puppy was moved, to Ma Balcooleh's utter amazement, Ma Johnson's house was in complete darkness and it looked like it had been deserted for days. She suddenly felt light-headed and a surge of fear swept through her body. She firmly held the candle and stumbled into her house. She grabbed her rosary and said couple decades in quick succession and then fell into a restless sleep.

The next day Ma Balcooleh noticed the mysterious bluish dark spots on her body and she quickly told her neighbor about them.

More people began seeing and hearing bizarre images and sounds at nights. One person said one night he saw his neighbor's house on fire but when he got closer to it, it was fine and there were no signs of fire. Another person said odd footsteps were heard on the roof of her house and yet another reported that she saw weird flickering lights in her fowl coop late one night.

Not only that -- the bizarre bluish dark spots began making their appearances on more people. Furthermore, a mysterious yellow fungus-like thing was seen under many houses.

The different stories all trickled down and formed one big story and it was then everyone realized that the area was being haunted at nights by a soukouyan.

Panic gripped the place and everyone began to build defenses against their nightly guest. People bought horse shoes and nailed them upside down in their houses. Crucifixes were made from bwa dyab and placed over windows and doors. Others bought Jayes to scrub their houses and sprinkle in their yards while some took nightly baths of garlic and zèb kouwès (snake grass). Some burnt tires in their yards and many took the religious route and said novenas and offered masses in churches all over Dominica.

But the soukouyan seemed unstoppable as night after night people heard abnormal noises, saw astonishing lights, had more bluish dark spots over their bodies and the now-familiar yellow fungus-like thing under their houses, which was later revealed to be the feces of the soukouyan.

But then news broke that would strike even more fear in the hearts of the people. And that was the news that a powerful hurricane, called Hurricane David, was heading towards Dominica.

The news was sketchy because, at that time, only DBS Radio was accessible island wide on the 595 AM band. Some people tuned in to Voice Of Barbados to get information but nothing much was coming from that station either, so most people simply tied down their galvanize roofs with rope and prayed for the best.

The night before the hurricane struck Avandale ignored the warnings given on DBS Radio and went and sat instead under the mango tree waiting for the soukouyan to make its appearance in Marie Galante. And it did not disappoint.

Like clockwork, the boukan appeared and began leaping in all directions. After its display, the soukouyan headed to Dominica as it usually did but the hurricane was also getting closer and closer to Dominica.

Avandale was not sure what was going on but apparently the soukouyan was unaware that the hurricane was so close to Dominica. At roughly 3 a.m., the storm caught up with it as it made its way across the ocean to the island.

Avandale watched in amazement as the ball of flame, that was the soukouyan, was tossed around by the storm. Sometimes it went way up in the sky and other times it looked like it would be plunged into the dark waters of the Atlantic. For about half an hour the spectacular show continued until the hurricane enveloped the soukouyan and the ball of flame disappeared completely.

The next day was August 29, 1979 and Hurricane David struck Dominica with all its fury. Despite the devastation many people in the area were grateful: they credited it for destroying the soukouyan from Marie Galante.

The House that Baptiste Built

For many years, Baptiste was the most popular person around although there were many strange stories that swirled around him. Maybe because he was such a generous person who was well known around the area that no one really wanted to believe anything "bad" about him.

Very little or nothing was known about Baptiste's past. What was well known was that he had gone to England in the late 50s and it is said that while there he won some kind of lottery, took the money and returned to Dominica. That was about it.

What was well known was the fact that upon his return, Baptiste bought a piece of secluded land, surrounded it with a high fence and started to build his house. It was a project that would consume the rest of his life.

Of course, there were rumors that the house went up rather quickly although he hired virtually no one to work for him. But no one paid attention to any of this because since Baptiste's return from England he had become very popular in the area: he gave children sweetie on their way to school; he paid for funerals and weddings; he helped with school tuitions; was very popular at the rum shop since he generously bought rum for everyone and was always present at Nine Nights and wakes.

But somehow there were many things about Baptiste that gave reasons for the arousal of suspicion. For example, no one had actually ever seen Baptiste on the road at nights despite the fact that he was always at Nine Nights or wakes or at the rum shop. He would just suddenly appear from behind a bush or from underneath the house or from behind the kitchen. What people saw before Baptiste appeared was a dog or a cow and occasionally, a rooster. But since these animals were common in the area, no one thought much of it.

During one Nine Night, somebody said he saw a big black dog disappear behind a clump of plantain trees and, a minute later

Baptiste emerged and the dog was never seen again. But Baptiste bought a half bottle of rum for the person who saw this and the incident was forgotten promptly.

Another person said that he saw Baptiste naked at a crossroad at midnight "on four legs like a dog with his bottom in the air." The person said he was so scared he immediately ran away but no one believed the story.

But probably the most compelling story concerning Baptiste came from Alphonse. Late one night Alphonse said he was going home after a night of heavy drinking. Thinking that the road home was too long, he decided to go across Baptiste's property as a form of a short cut. So he found a hole in the fence and stumbled along to his home.

He was approaching Baptiste's house when he heard something which sounded like the rubbing of oars in a boat. He quickly hid behind a bush and to his amazement he saw a boat, in mid-air, floating out of the darkness. On board, were ten dog-like men, which Alphonse later said were lougawous. The boats floated pass him landed in front of Baptiste's doorstep and the lougawous climbed out.

Baptiste came out of his house, greeted them and they immediately set to work on the house. From his hiding point Alphonse remained frozen both in fear and amazement as the lougawous worked on Baptiste's house and after a couple of hours, Baptiste and the ten lougawous entered his house.

After a couple of minutes eleven dog-like men emerged, climbed into the boat and the boat disappeared into the darkness. Alphonse remained hidden, frozen in his hiding spot until he got the energy to run home in great fear. He told everyone who would listen what he saw and said that Baptiste was a lougawou but no one believed Alphonse's story because they say he was drunk and maybe some la diabless was playing tricks on him.

Despite this compelling story, it was reduced to a tool used by parents to frighten misbehaving boys who would say to them, "if all you doh behave all you self, we will call Alphonse lougawou to bite all you toelee."

Baptiste's house continued to go up at a rapid pace for several months and then without warning, he became dreadfully ill and was taken to the hospital in a deep coma.

Everyone was baffled and could not understand what happen to their benefactor until one of Baptiste's few workers told one of the most incredible stories that were ever to be heard in that part of Dominica.

The story was told by a fellah who everyone called Passit.

According to Passit, Baptiste had become very obsessed with the construction of his house and was exploring every possible avenue to have it completed. Passit said he heard Baptiste had used lougawous to assist but one day he came up with the most twisted of all schemes: he decided to hatch a 'ti dyab' or what some people called a 'bolom.'

To do this Baptiste bought some white chicken and waited until one laid an egg on Good Friday. Baptiste placed the egg under his left arm until it hatched but what was hatched was no chicken but a bolom which Passit said look like a tiny man or dwarf. The bolom grew by the hour and Passit said it was supposed to live for three days and within that three-day period it was to build Baptiste's house. But after the three days had transpired, greed overcame Baptiste and he refused to get rid of it. To make matters worse the bolom depended on Baptiste's blood to survive and as it grew it demanded more and more blood.

Passit said many a night he heard Baptiste and the bolom in fierce struggles inside the house but still he refused to get rid of it. One night the bolom sucked so much of his blood, he fell into a deep coma and had to be rushed to the hospital.

No one knew where the bolom went after that since Baptiste could no longer feed it, but people said it would always have its revenge somehow.

Baptiste eventually recovered, however, there was one room in the house that Baptiste built which could never be completed because every year a strange mysterious force demolished it. This happened no matter how many times the room was rebuilt.

And people said it was the bolom taking its revenge.

Tax and the Cemetery Spirit

The night began rather simple enough. Tax drank his normal shot of zayid, took a long drink of water to chase it and headed to bed.

The night was mingled with sounds that Tax was familiar with: the wind in the kenip tree, the chirp of crickets, dogs barked continuously and somewhere a mabouya croaked in the banana field behind the house.

The usual sounds lulled Tax into a peaceful sleep but halfway through the night he suddenly began dreaming of his father. In the dream, his father wore a black suit and a white top hat. He had a wooden cane in his hands. Then his father began raining blows mercilessly on him with the cane.

Tax twisted and writhed with pain as his father plummeted him with the cane. He tried to scream but nothing came from his mouth. He tried to resist but his entire body had turned to lead. After what seemed an eternity, he awoke from the dream with a weak scream emitting from his mouth. He was covered with sweat and his body ached.

When Tax's father was alive, they never had a good relationship. His father thought Tax was lazy and Tax thought his father drank too much. Sometimes the two went on no-talking terms for years and even on his death bed his father's heart remained cold.

Following his father's death, Tax sunk into a state of depression, saddened by the fact that he and his father had never made peace between them. He went on long drinking sprees and sometimes would burst into tears for no apparent reason. But he had never dreamt of his father, until tonight. That, Tax thought was very strange.

Tax pondered the dream throughout the next day and wondered what it meant. He was so deep in thought that he didn't realize the day was done and night had taken on its task of covering the land with darkness.

He went to fetch his bottle of zayid but to his utter amazement, it was empty. Baffled, Tax thought hard. He knew that the last time he drank from it the bottle, it was half full. And that was last night. He went to sit on his bed, trying to make sense of this occurrence. He thought hard. Maybe Balla had sneaked into his house and drank the rum. Balla was his best friend and was known to sneak into Tax's house to help himself to various treats. Or probably he did drink all of it because sometimes whenever he started on the bottle, one drink led to the next. But he remembered drinking only one shot.

Still deep in thought, Tax decided to call it a day and went to bed. He was drifting into sleep when he heard it. It was someone calling his name in a whisper. "Tax, Tax." Twice. The sound of the whisper was mechanical, devoid of emotion or purpose. It sounded as if it was just within the range of hearing and you would have heard it only if you were listening carefully.

Tax did not answer and concentrated on falling asleep.

The whisper did not repeat itself although the sound of it reverberated through his head.

Then without warning, cold fear swept through his body. He jumped from the bed and although he felt cold, he realized he was sweating profusely. Then without warning, there was a loud crash in the living room followed by the sound of shattering glass. Gathering his senses Tax rushed towards the direction of the sound and what he saw filled him with utter disbelief.

Lying on the floor with its frame shattered, was the portrait of Tax's father. That portrait has been hanging in the same spot on the wall for as long as he remembered and it had never fallen down. The sight of it lying on the floor covered with glass from the frame filled him with a combination of fear and curiosity.

But matters were to deteriorate.

A couple of nights later Tax was heading to bed when he heard a thump behind the house. The sound was barely audible, almost like something from a dream. It stopped and Tax dismissed it as something from his imagination.

Feeling a bit unsettled, he arranged the bed and stretched out on it. The sound came again, slightly louder this time. One, two, three times and then again, it stopped. Tax tried to figure out what the sound was. He thought it sounded like a cow stamping its hoof against the hard ground or someone grinding coffee in a mortar. He listened carefully, straining his ears but the thumping sound had stopped. Again he dismissed it and tried to fall asleep but as he was drifting into slumber the sound exploded right below the window. Tax got up swiftly. He flung the window open hoping to see what the source of the sound was.

The cool night-wind danced over his face. He peered through the darkness, straining his eyes but could see nothing. It was then he got the creepy feeling that there was someone in the room. Frozen to the spot where he stood, Tax could feel the hair on his neck rising and he felt a blast of cold air hitting his body.

Slowly, ever so slowly, he turned around from the window and what greeted his eyes filled him with horror. Standing across the room was his father. He wore the same white suit he was buried in and in his hand he held his favorite instrument he used to punish Tax as a child: a guava branch.

And then Tax felt terribly drowsy. The ground beneath him swayed to the right and swayed to the left. The last thing he remembered was his feet turning to jelly.

When he regained his senses the sun had already risen and someone was knocking at his door. It was Balla who he had promised $20.

"Man, you looking like you just see a jumbie," Balla said when Tax opened the door. So Tax told Balla of the night occurrences and the other inexplicable things that he had been experiencing. Balla listened intently and said, "Garcon you better go and make a round eh, you better go and make a round."

Tax knew going to make "a round" meant paying a visit to an obeah man. At first, he was skeptical but the look on Balla's face was enough to convince him. He began making plans in his head to visit an obeah man and to get some insights into what was taking place and its relationship to his father.

That night, following Balla's suggestion, Tax sprinkled some holy water around the house, washed the front step with Jays and hung a rosary on the door. Before he went to bed he said a couple of Psalms and said some prayers from an old prayer book his mother gave him many, many years ago. Then he turned his clothes inside out and went to bed.

Two weeks later, the night was quiet and a thin moon hung in the dark sky. Tax followed the obeah man's instructions carefully. He was told that he should wait when the first quarter of the moon was a little bit over the horizon, probably around 11:00 pm. Then he would be ready to do what he was supposed to do.

First, he rubbed himself with Oil of Man and lit a black candle in each corner of his house. Then he wrote his father's name and his own name on a small piece of parchment paper, wrapped it carefully and placed it under his arm. Then put on his clothes inside out, went outside and sprinkled Stay Away Powder in a circle around the house. Then he went underneath the house in the darkness and waited for what was haunting him to turn up.

According to the obeah man, Tax's father had died with hatred in his heart and that hatred had attracted an evil spirit who was, in turn, using his father's spirit to haunt him. The obeah man's disclosure had baffled Tax, and that day he walked around Roseau in deep thought as he bought the various things he was told to buy.

The thin moon dodged between clouds, casting eerie shadows all over the place and Tax held on firmly to the bag with the whip the obeah man had given him. He did not know what the whip was made of but it smelled strongly of garlic, alkali and tabak zombie. For Tax it was his only defense from the unknown.

A thump down the road jerked him from his thoughts and Tax peered through the dim moonlight. The thumping grew louder and louder and something appeared that sent chills down his spine. It was a horse, a white horse.

Tax stared in disbelief as the animal walked slowly and deliberately to this house. The moon ducked behind a cloud and the white horse seemed to merge into the darkness but suddenly it stopped. Tax knew it had reached the line of Stay Away Powder that was protecting his house.

The horse huffed, puffed and stamped its hoof as if annoyed. It went behind the house as if searching for an opening in the Stay Away Powder defense but found none. It released a long loud snort and turned around in the direction it came.

Tax knew it was the evil spirit the obeah man had told him about and it was heading back to the cemetery where his father's body was buried.

Tax emerged from under the house and followed. The obeah man had told him he had to go to the cemetery where he was to face the evil spirit and "put it in it place" once and for all.

The night was unusually cool and quiet. The moon continued its game of hide and seek with the clouds with dark shadows dancing all over the place. Filled with a combination of curiosity and confidence, Tax felt unafraid. He held on to the bag with the whip firmly. He checked his pocket to make sure the bottle of holy water was in its place.

He followed the horse through the dark, keeping it just within the range of sight. In the silent night, he could hear the gentle thud of its hoof on the pitch of the road. And then suddenly the Catholic church loomed over him in the dark. He had reached his destination because the cemetery was located behind the church.

The obeah man had warned that a powerful spirit guarded all cemeteries and there were some things he had to do in order for him to enter undetected. So reaching into his pocket Tax pulled out the small bag of dirt. The dirt was gathered at a crossroad at midnight a couple of nights ago. He poured three handfuls of the dirt over his head, spun around three times, then spat at the four corners of the Earth. He then made ten signs of the cross and spun around three more times. And he was ready to enter the cemetery.

The horse was nowhere to be seen and darkness covered the cemetery since the moon had hidden itself. Tax made his way to his father's grave. He was just within eyesight of it when his blood suddenly turned cold. Sitting on his father's grave was something that looked like the dark figure of a man. The figure's head was bowed as if in prayer and it was unmoving.

Instinctively Tax ducked behind the closest grave and peered around it. The figure remained where it was and he began creeping closer to his father's grave.

The obeah man had told him he needed to strike whatever he saw in the cemetery at least three times with the whip in order to 'put it in it place.' Holding his breath Tax crept closer and closer to the figure and the grave and by accident, he stepped on a twig.

In the silence, the snapping of the twig sounded like an exploding bomb. He was momentarily confused and when he regained his senses, to his utter disbelief the figure on the grave had disappeared.

Just then he heard rustling behind him and he spun around. Towering over him was the dark figure and before he could react, he felt a blow to his right side. The force of the blow sent him spinning and he rolled over one grave and the next. When he came to a stop he felt the same terrible sense of drowsiness he felt back at his home the night he heard the spirit. The earth swayed to the left and then to the right. Huge dark shapes appeared before his eyes and he wished he could find a bed to collapse in.

In the confusion of his mind, he remembered what the obeah man told him. He reached into his pocket and grabbed the bottle of holy water. He sprinkled the liquid in the direction of the spirit and in the silence he heard dull groans. The holy water was hitting its mark.

Tax struggled to his feet and peered through the darkness. As if part of a conspiracy against him, the moon remained hidden behind a cloud. Now he could barely see anything. He pulled the whip from the bag. The smell of garlic and alkali and tabak zombie filled his nostril. Regaining strength, he moved towards the grave.

Once again he saw the spirit. It was moving towards him. Tax felt unafraid and he swung the whip. A scream ripped through the dark and he swung again. Feeling a burst of adrenaline Tax swung and swung the whip at the dark figure. Scream after scream followed and then abruptly it stopped.

Then with a burst of energy, Tax turned and fled the cemetery. He ran like he had never run before.

His house was quiet and the black candles were burning low. He tumbled into bed and instantly fell into a deep slumber.

Tax never dreamt his father again and he knew the old man was resting in peace.

However, after that, he made sure every year, on All Saint's Day, he lit a candle on his father's grave.

Rufus and the La Diabless

Excitement was in the air, the annual domino competition was about to begin and everyone who could walk or crawl had gathered at Mr. Nwell's shop for the occasion. Thick tobacco smoke and the smell of rum permeated the air. In the corner of the shop, a heap of speakers blared old calypsos.

But everyone's eyes were set on the bouko or rum barrel that Mr. Nwell bought once a year for the occasion. The barrel was opened with great ceremony before the competition began and it was Rufus' job to draw the rum from it with a hose. Every time Rufus drew some rum from the barrel, he sneaked in a mouth full and within a couple of hours, he was drunk. As expected, he would end up on the corner half-smiling.

Rufus was on his fifth draw from the bouko and the domino competition was well on its way. Feeling a bit tipsy he decided to go outside for some fresh air. Outside, the night was cool and there were dark shadows everywhere. And it was then, between the shadows, Rufus saw the dog. He would later say that he had never seen the dog before and could not remember it belonging to anyone in the area.

The dog was probably the most beautiful animal he had ever seen, with large ears and a bushy tail. He swore the eyes shone pale red.

Suddenly Rufus felt numb, his hair stood on edge and a great wave of fear briefly swept over him. "Is the rum you know," he muttered to himself. "I getting too old for that eh."

He decided to join the other excited people in the shop but there was something attractive about the dog, something he could not explain or comprehend.

And then Rufus decided to do something that he never did before: go home in the middle of a domino competition. It was a mortal sin doing this since veteran domino players always said that a player never leaves a game in the night when that game is incomplete.

The next day a search party was formed when Rufus was not found at his home. He was found later in the day shivering in a patch of zéb kouto (razor grass) and taken home. Rufus recovered only after he was given sugar water to drink and was rubbed from head to toe with Red Lavender and snake oil.

Then he told a strange story of what happened to him.

According to Rufus, he was on his way home on the dark road when he heard a clip-clop sound behind him. "It was like a donkey, I telling all you," he said. "And I feel as if something or somebody was following me. I doh take that for nothing but the more I walk the more I hear the noise behind me."

Then Rufus said out of nowhere a beautiful Indian woman appeared and was standing in front of him. "I doh know where the Indian come out eh, I telling all you," he related. "But she was in front me, just so. A pretty Indian woman eh, nice long hair, pretty man, pretty."

He said without uttering a word, the Indian woman grabbed his hand and he followed blindly feeling contented in the thought that he was going to make love to her. "But I doh remember nothing again," he stated, scratching his head in puzzlement. "I maybe fall asleep because is all you that wake me up."

And everyone began to say that Rufus was a victim of a la diabless, a mischievous jumbie that likes to prey on drunk and weak-headed men who cannot refuse beautiful women. But Rufus was convinced the Indian woman was real and it was the rum that was playing tricks on him.

Some months later Mr. Nwell was hosting a jimp ping dance at his shop and Rufus dressed up to attend the event. He purchased his usual half bottle of rum and went to sit in a corner to admire the dancers.

He was on his fourth or fifth drink when he saw the dog again but then it vanished and in its place, the Indian woman was seen standing in its place behind some hibiscus bushes. Excitement swept through him. He was convinced that the woman had come to meet him again.

"I must get you tonight eh," Rufus said under his breath but he had to take two more shots of rum before he could muster the courage to go and talk to the woman.

He made his way through the dancers and into the yard but to his utter amazement when he got to the place where the Indian woman was standing, she was nowhere to be seen.

Discombobulated, Rufus looked around and he saw the Indian woman but on the opposite side of the yard, halfway hidden in the darkness.

He could not understand how she got there so quickly but nonetheless he crossed the yard again to meet her. The same thing occurred. By the time he got on the other side of the yard, the Indian woman was back in her original position. This went on for about an hour but somehow Rufus could not stop and it seemed as if he was consumed by some invisible power to continue the cat and mouse-like game.

Suddenly the Indian woman came over to him provocatively, motioning for a dance. He gleefully joined her and Rufus danced like he had never danced before.

The next day the whole area was abuzz with Rufus' strange behavior at the dance. They said for hours Rufus crisscrossed the yard as if looking for someone and muttering to himself. They further stated that he eventually joined the other dancers and it appeared that he was dancing with someone but he was all alone.

Then Rufus became ill and again he was rubbed with Red Lavender and snake oil. He was also given a bath of garlic, glory cedar leaves, man-better-man leaves, and other concoctions. Gradually, he got better.

Another night Rufus was on his way to a wake when again, he ran into the Indian woman. They walked together along the road without speaking to each other but Rufus could not help but hear the clip-clopping sound he heard the first time he met her.

He wanted to ask the woman about the source of the sound and ask her name but his tongue became suddenly heavy and he realized he could not say a word.

Then Rufus remembered Mr. Nwell's advice about what he should do when he met the Indian woman again. He slowly rolled his left sleeve three times and reached into his pocket for the small bottle of holy water and garlic that was given to him. Before he could pull them out of his pocket, the Indian woman grabbed his hand firmly.

Rufus pulled away and grabbed his flashlight. He turned it on and flashed it at his mysterious companion. To his utter horror, the first thing he saw was that the Indian woman had only one human leg, the other was that of a donkey. In an instant, everything became pitch black.

Rufus never really recovered and he died some days later, but he gained enough strength to whisper his last encounter with the Indian woman.

The following day Mr. Nwell led an entourage to the huge bamboo grove near the health center and burnt it down. They then spread holy water all over the area. When they were leaving they threw three handfuls of dirt behind them and never looked back till they arrived at the shop.

And the la diabless was never seen in the area again.

Mabel and the de Laurence ring

When she saw it, she should have turned her head and go along her merry way, but Mabel was not that kind of person. She lived by the philosophy of "whatever dog get on ground is dog own," so without thinking twice she picked it up and slipped it into her pocket.

When Mabel found it, 'de Laurence' was beginning to get popular in Dominica and there were whispers that a certain obeah man on the east coast had in his possession the feared "Sixth and Seventh Books of Moses" and was using them to further his skills. It was said he had gotten the book from de Laurence.

But this was far from Mabel's mind when she got home to examine her prize. It was a ring; unlike what she had ever seen before. The top of the ring was flat and engraved with two circles. Between the circles, strange writings and symbols protruded from the ring. In the middle was something that looked like the head of a dog or wolf, she was not sure. The ring was heavy and felt cold to the touch and she was not sure whether it was gold or not.

Mabel placed the ring in the old suitcase in which she kept valuables, pushed the suitcase under the bed and went to do her house chores. But she began to feel a sensation as if someone was in the house watching her. She could feel the eyes on her back and it felt so real that whenever she turned around, she expected to see someone there. She looked through the whole house but as usual, it was all empty. Mabel lived alone.

Seeing no one, she thought maybe old age was catching up with her, so she called one of the neighbor's children and sent him to the shop for a gill of cask rum. That would shift her perception a bit, she thought. As expected, the effect of the rum warmed her stomach and she no longer felt as if someone was in the house.

That evening after sending the neighbor's child to the shop on two more rum runs, Mabel sat down to listen to the radio until she fell asleep. She woke up later on and headed to her bed. Although she had just installed electricity in her house, she still preferred the warm glow of her kerosene lamp and this she lit before hitting the pillows.

She was just about to drift into slumber when she heard the weird sound. It was unfamiliar, like the slow dripping of water in a deep well. Mabel sat up in the bed, trying to locate the source of the sound but she could not -- sometimes it seemed as if it was coming from under the bed and sometimes from somewhere outside.

Cursing under her breath Mabel went outside to examine the old drum she used for catching rainwater, but it was empty. Amazed, she reentered the house. Interestingly the sound was gone but then again, she got the overwhelming sensation that someone was in the house.

"But what is that," Mabel said to herself. "Somebody I know die man and I doh know yet. But who I know that sick to die nuh? I doh know nobody."

Convinced that a relative had died and the spirit had come to alert her, she made a sign of the cross and muttered, "May the souls of the faithful departed rest in peace, amen."

She fell asleep and dreamt she was hosting a dance in her yard and there were Mazouk, Quadrille and Bèlè dancers. The whole area rang with the sound of tanbou bèlè, boom-boom and accordion. Since she was good at Heel and Toe Polka, Mabel dreamt she danced and danced until she was completely exhausted.

Next day Mabel woke up tired and sweaty. As she got out of bed she caught the glimpse of someone's fleeting shadow in the direction of the kitchen. She stumbled after the shadow, convinced that she was going to catch a thief but when she got to the kitchen, there was no one there.

As she stood in the kitchen, Mabel felt suddenly chilly. She felt someone standing near her and she shuddered violently. She stumbled out of the kitchen and into the yard only to run into Ma Terez, her friend.

"What happened nuh?" Ma Terez asked her. "You looking sick and tired."

Mabel smiled and said she was fine.

"So when you having your dance you not thinking of me eh," Ma Terez stated.

"What you talking about nuh?" Mabel asked.

Ma John proceeded to tell Mabel of how she stayed from her yard and saw Mabel hosting a dance with the Bèlè, Quadrille and Mazouk dancers and how the dance went into the early hours of the morning.

Baffled Mabel said she did not host any dance at her home but Ma Terez insisted and the two finally settled on an uneasy truce about this matter.

Then more strange things began happening at Mabel's home. One day she could not find her bible although it never left her room. She found it couple of days later under the breadfruit tree in the yard with many pages torn from it.

One of the neighbor's children told her that he saw a white man sunbathing on her roof but Mabel did not believe the story until an adult told her he also saw the same white man.

She heard rattling in the kitchen and although she placed rat poison all over the place she never saw a single dead rat. And the rat poison remained untouched.

The sound of the dripping water was heard every night and Mabel could not find the source.

But what pushed Mabel to take action was the day she actually saw the white man her neighbors spoke to her about.

She was in the yard weeding and when she took a break and looked up, there in the window was the man.

Mabel dropped her cutlass and fled, straight to Ma Terez's yard.

The very next day, following Ma Terez counsel, Mabel decided to visit the obeah man. She was told her somebody was "trying a thing" on her so she better go and "look out for yourself."

So she went and told the obeah man everything that had been happening at her home from the time she found the strange ring. When she showed the ring to the obeah man, he almost jumped out of his chair.

"Let me tell you something eh," he said. "That ring there is something you should not have eh. You should never have take that ring from where it was. The owner at your home right now. Is a de Laurence ring I telling you. I going take the ring but you have to make the owner leave your house. Now listen to me carefully."

That night it was very dark and Mabel walked swiftly down the road. She glanced nervously over her shoulders since she heard footsteps behind her. She wanted to make sure she arrived at the crossroads at the stroke of midnight just as she was instructed by the obeah man. She broke into a run as she heard the footsteps grow louder and louder behind her.

She arrived at the crossroad and quickly grabbed three handfuls of dirt. This she poured over her head and headed back home. On her way home, she noticed the footsteps had stopped and it was oddly quiet. The obeah man had told her that when she poured three handfuls of dirt from the crossroad on her head at exactly midnight, she would be actually 'underground' and would be invisible to everything, including spirits.

Mabel went home and slept peacefully for the first time in a long time and this was the first step in getting rid of a spirit that came with the de Laurence ring.

The next day, following the obeah man's instructions, she went to the seaside, counted seven waves and after the seventh wave, she filled a hand basin with seawater. This she took home and placed under the bed. Then Mabel went to the Catholic church and got a bottle of holy water. She took this home and mixed it with the sea water in the basin that was under her bed. The mixture was left for three days under the bed away from the rays of the sun. On the third day, Mabel threw in snake oil, red lavender, and a variety of foul smelling oils given to her by the obeah man.

Then she wrote her name on a piece of goat skin given to her by the obeah man, folded it into seven folds and dipped it three times into the mixture. She placed the paper on the sill of the window that was facing west. She settled down and anxiously waited for nightfall. Tonight she was going to drive away the spirit from her house once and for all.

Night fell quickly and when it was close to midnight Mabel sprang into action. The obeah man told her she had to be quick, to catch the spirit off guard. She quickly turned off her kerosene lamp and lit the black candle she had bought in Roseau. Then she grabbed the hand basin and was about to start sprinkling the strange mixture on her bed when she heard a loud crash coming from the direction of the kitchen. The obeah man told her she should not be deterred by anything, so she went ahead and sprinkled her bed, then all the parts of her room.

She was about to enter the living room when she heard the sound of someone jumping on the galvanized roof. The sound was deafening and Mable feared her neighbors would hear the racket, come over to investigate and throw her plans off track.

She quickly continued sprinkling the mixture all over the house and she did the same outside. Then she threw what was left of the mixture to the four corners of the earth and went back to her room.

The black candle burnt steadily, the noise on the roof stopped. Then, there was a loud sound outside; like that of a breadfruit falling on hard ground. Silence followed.

Mabel fell asleep and she slept like she never did before. From that time onwards, she never picked up anything she knew did not belong to her.

How Petite and Heskit Killed a Soukouyan

Very few people saw the mysterious light the first time because it all started happening late at night. Those who saw it said what looked like a flashlight suddenly appeared in the sky up north in the direction of Portsmouth. It bobbed up and down a couple of times and like a shooting star it shot its way rapidly across the sky into the direction of Ma John's mango tree.

No one remembered what happened next because the witnesses to the mysterious light were suddenly overwhelmed by deep sleep as if anesthetized, and had to retire immediately to bed.

So night after night different people witnessed the same phenomena and no one could understand what was really going on.

Then around the time these things began happening, people started to see a difference in Ma John. She used to be quite jovial, a person who cracked jokes with people, laughed at her own jokes and would never refuse a good shot of spice rum. "It good for your belly eh," she would always say. On Sundays she would sit under the mango tree with her best friend Madonn and gossip about everyone around, both of them emitting shrill bursts of laughter.

But all that changed. Ma John turned suddenly hostile and unfriendly. She no longer ran to the shop for a shot of spice rum, she refused to greet people on the road and most importantly, to Madonn's chagrin, the Sunday afternoon gossip sessions came to an abrupt end.

People were baffled by this transformation.

What was even more baffling was the day Ma John ran into Madonn by the river and boldly told her former friend that she was using her favorite washing stone. And within the blink of an eye, the two flew at each other with flailing hands. Those who were at the river dropped whatever they were doing and rush to the scene shouting, "Woman fighting. Action. Action. Hegas, hegas."

The news of the fight between the two former best friends spread through the area like a wildfire. Of course, people began to wonder more and more what was really happening to Ma John.

And then many things began happening in the area. First of all, people noticed that students began performing poorly at school. Either they were not interested in their school work, would be sleepy all the time or have a general laissez-faire attitude. Many complained of being tired all the time and then discernible dark spots began surfacing all over their bodies.

That was just the beginning. One very dark night Heskit was just about to fall asleep when he heard a loud raucous in the fowl house. Always on a look out for snakes, which occasionally preyed on his chicken, he grabbed his flashlight and flung open the window. And in the yard he saw a hen, followed by about five chicks, clucking along merrily.

Heskit was very intrigued by this since he knew chickens and darkness don't mix but thought it probably belonged to a neighbor (he knew the hen did not belong to him because he had never seen it before).

He grabbed some clothes and rushed outside with the intention of keeping it and its brood till morning and then he would locate its owner.

But in the yard, the hen and the chicks were nowhere to be found. Heskit searched under the house, in the kitchen, even in the outhouse but it was to no avail. When he went to the fowl-house, all his chickens were fast asleep and no sign of recent disturbance was evident.

Then Heskit felt suddenly weak, his head felt as if it was growing rapidly. His legs turned to rubber. He held on to the fowl-house for support while shivers ran up and down his spine from the atlas to the coccyx. He felt cold. Thinking that he was probably having a heart attack, he tried to scream but his tongue was heavy in his mouth and only a squeak emanated from it.

It was then he saw the orange glow coming from the direction of Ma John's house. He watched in fascination as the glow grew bright, became weak, grew bright again and continued the cycle over and over again.

Heskit was not sure how long he stood there but slowly he felt the energy flowing through his legs again and despite the lingering fear in him, he was overwhelmed by curiosity. He decided to investigate the source of the orange glow as best as he could.

From the vantage point in his yard, he gasped in disbelief at what he saw. On the mango tree in Ma John's yard was someone holding what looked like a kerosene torch of brousai. From where he was, Heskit could not recognize the person, but the flame from the brousai leaped here and there, casting eerie shadows all over the yard. Then he saw someone looking like Ma John running from the mango tree to the house.

The brousai on the mango tree abruptly dimmed and turned to what looked like the light of a flashlight and the person holding it appeared to be climbing higher into the tree. Suddenly the thing stopped its ascent and Heskit felt a wave of fear sweeping over him. He dropped his flashlight, turned and ran to his house. But he did not get far for his legs turned to rubber again and he fainted.

Then many things began happening to Heskit. First, he noticed that he was weak and without energy in the mornings. He felt lazy throughout the day and his garden suffered tremendously.

Then he began hearing strange shuffling sounds under his house and a bizarre scrape on the roof every night around midnight. And there were the dark-bluish spots all over his body. In order to battle the weakness, he was feeling, someone told him to drink Ferrol and Seven Seas Cod Liver Oil but none of these helped. He even took baths of Glory Cedar, Patjouli, and Bay Leaf and that too did not help.

Then he began having very strange dreams. In the dreams, he was always falling through a bottomless abyss and Ma John was the one who always pushed him in. He would wake up on the floor, sweating profusely, without realizing he had fallen from his bed.

So one day he related his whole experience to his friend Petit and to his great surprise they shared similar experiences. Petite showed him the dark-bluish spot on his body and told of the constant fatigue he felt. And Petite said many people in the area were experiencing the same thing. Eventually, the conversation turned to Ma John and Petite said he too had seen the strange glow coming from her yard but he had not thought much of it since Ma John was always burning leaves habitually, ritualistically.

Ma John's behavior got worse and was on everyone's lips. But what left people in the area searching for answers was the incident at church. Ma John was a devout Catholic and went to church every Sunday and holy days of obligation. That particular Sunday she was in the line for communion but when she approached the priest, the chalice flew out of his hands as if slapped violently by someone. The little white hosts flew in a thousand directions. A look of terror appeared on the priest's face and he shouted, "Evil, evil is in the house of the Lord." Mass ended abruptly that day and no one really knew what to make of this peculiar incident.

But Heskit was convinced that Ma John had become a soukouyan and something had to be done about it. He spoke to Petite of his conviction and told of his plan to visit a gardeh for instructions. That day they made a pact between them that they would get rid of whatever had become of Ma John.

About a week later, on a dark moonless night, Heskit and Petite were lying flat on their stomachs in the banana field next to Ma John's house. Both men wore their clothes inside out and back to front with rosaries and pendants of St. Mark the Lion around their necks. Petite held a fish gun with a spear of stainless steel that had been rubbed with garlic, alkali and horse urine. Heskit held an ancient rifle and a small bag filled with bullets that had also been rubbed with the same things as the spear.

Upon Heskit's signal, Petite crept from their hiding place and made his way to Ma John's kitchen, which was a galvanize shack separate from her house.

Petite groped his way through the thick darkness and entered the kitchen which had an even darker interior. With his heart beating loudly he placed a jar of sand next to the pillon (mortar) that was in the kitchen. Soukouyans normally placed their skins in a pillon for the night while they went flying on their expeditions but on their return, a jar of sand nearby normally tempted them to count all the sand before putting their skins back on. While the soukouyan was distracted by its sand counting, Heskit and Petite agreed they would strike.

Petite was about to head back to their hiding place to await the return of the soukouyan when without warning a bright yellow light filled the yard, shattering the darkness. He panicked and broke into a run but he felt a sharp pain behind his head and he fell into a heap.

From their hiding place, Heskit was surprised by a sudden burst of light. The soukouyan had returned without warning and he feared for Petite.

Grabbing the rifle, he burst from the hiding place and ran in the direction of the kitchen. When he turned the corner around the house, what Heskit saw filled him with horror.

On the ground lay Petite. Standing over him was what looked like a giant torch, with flames leaping all over. Standing in the middle of the flames was someone who looked like Ma John, except that she was red all over as if someone had peeled her skin off. In her hand, she held a broom. She raised the broom in order to strike the limp body on the ground.

"Petite, Petite," Heskit screamed.

The creature froze with the broom suspended in mid-air. Then it turned around and began walking towards Heskit, slowly and deliberately, flames dancing in its wake. It covered the short ground that separated them in no time.

As the soukouyan drew closer, Heskit could see its face and it was not the face of Ma John. The face was skinless, with small amounts of blood oozing out from spots here and there. The eyes were like the eyes of a snake, except they were red and bloodshot. They glowed slightly, like the light of a weak flashlight. The whole countenance of the face was the countenance of evil, and there was a sneer on it. It was a sneer that sent shivers down his spine.

Heskit wanted to turn and run, but he found no energy. He felt weak in the legs and he began backing away from the advancing soukouyan, more by instinct than anything else. He wanted to scream to Petite, but he could not find his voice. The more he backed up, the more the thing in front of him got closer.

Suddenly his foot hit something. It was a piece of wood and he found himself stumbling backward. He rolled over and over again.

"Petite, Petite," the words flew out of his throat as if by magic. "Petite, Petite."

Petite lay on the ground as if he was in a dream, as if he was floating in outer space. He heard someone calling his name, but it sounded far away. Who could it be? It sounded urgent, like someone in great distress.

"Petite, Petite."

Slowly, ever so slowly Petite's consciousness began returning and the sound of his name reverberated louder and louder. A flood of memories flashed raced through his head: Heskit; the banana field; the soukouyan. Then he remembered. He tried to sit up and found it hard to do so. He felt weak and drowsy. He looked in the direction where his name was being called, and what he saw made shivers run up and down his spine.

Heskit lay on the ground screaming his name. The soukouyan stood over him, raining blows with the broomstick. Occasionally a kick was added. There were occasional grunts as the blows found their mark.

Petite felt the energy flowing into him. He saw the fish gun leaning against the house, exactly where he had left it. He began thinking that he should get it and end what was happening. Slowly he got to his feet, the sound of his name and the grunts of Heskit loud in his ears. He found himself staggering and he felt weak, but he kept going, concentrating on the gun, brightly illuminated by the light of the soukouyan.

Petite grabbed the fish gun. Frantically he pulled on the rubber that would set the gun and send the spear to its target. The rubber was harder than ever and he realized he was shaking. He firmly placed the butt of the gun on his belly and continued pulling the rubber. He was concentrating so much on what he was doing; he did not realize that Heskit had stopped screaming. When he looked up, he saw the soukouyan coming in his direction, leaving a trail of dancing flames in its wake. He pulled the rubber even harder. Then it clicked into place.

Petite aimed the fish gun and the soukouyan froze. A brief moment of deathly silence followed. In the silence, he could hear the wild thumping of his heart. The two faced each other, like two adversaries in a fighting match. Both looked at each other intently. Petite never felt so scared in all his life, but he kept the gun pointed at the heart of the soukouyan, just as was instructed. He then pressed the trigger and the spear sped towards the soukouyan.

The spear hit the soukouyan slightly below the heart, instantly shattering three ribs and puncturing the lungs before being stopped by the vertebral column. Dark red blood began flowing out, pouring around the flames, but not extinguishing it and covering the ground around the soukouyan.

The soukouyan did not move. It just stood there, looking down at the spear protruding from its body, as if in a state of bewilderment. Suddenly it released a scream, a blood-curdling, piercing scream. The scream rang and rang in Petite's ears.

The soukouyan lifted itself from the ground and flew to the mango tree, leaving a trail of blood and flames (which had turned blue), behind it.

Petite ran towards Heskit and grabbed the rifle and took aim. He felt braver than ever. Although he knew the soukouyan was some distance away from him, he knew he would hit it. He pressed the trigger, and a loud explosion followed. The recoil of the rifle sent him flying and he landed on his back with a loud grunt. The soukouyan screamed again, this time weaker, with a gurgling sound.

The soukouyan lifted itself from the mango tree and flew away, bobbing up and down.

Darkness covered everything and silence followed. Petite crept towards Heskit who was still groaning on the ground.

Together they struggled to the banana field and collapsed.

The next day Ma John was found dead by the river. She had two of what the police described as stab wounds. Her death was eventually ruled a suicide.

But only Heskit and Petite knew what really happened and when they told the story many, many years later, when they were both old men, everyone knew that they were the only ones who had fought and killed a soukouyan and lived.

Glossary of Terms

Bèlè .... A traditional dance in Dominica

Boukan ......A bonfire

Bolom .... A small man brought in the world on Good Friday for evil intents

Brousai .....A kerosene torch common in the rural areas in the old days

Bwa Dyab .....Devil's Wood

Buoko......A wooden drum used for making and storing rum

Gadeh (gardè) .... A person who dabbles in obeah or other supernatural things

Glory Cedar......A tree said to have healing properties

Jumbie.....A spirit said to be common around Dominica

La Diabless ...A mischievous female jumbie that loves preying on men

La Feh Di Moun....End of the world. Judgement day.

Lalo ...... A huge firefly common in rural parts of Dominica

Lougawoo ...... A male witch, sometimes appearing in the form of a dog

Mabouya ....A small tree lizard

Mahoe Piman ..... A tree said to have some supernatural powers

Malfété ...... A person who use supernatural powers to do evil things

Mama Glo ....Mermaid

Mazouk ….. A traditional dance in Dominica

Patchouli …. A plant said to have healing powers

Pom Coolie ….. A plant said to have healing powers

Pilon …. A mortar used to pound coffee and the like

Quadrille ….. A traditional dance in Dominica

Soukouyan ….. A female witch

Tabak Zombie ….. Jumbie's Tobacco

Toelee …… A term commonly used to refer to the penis

Zayid ….. A moonshine-like type of rum made in rural Dominica

Zeb Kouwess …… Snake grass; a plant said to have healing properties

Zeb Kouto …… Razor grass

Made in the USA
Columbia, SC
04 November 2024